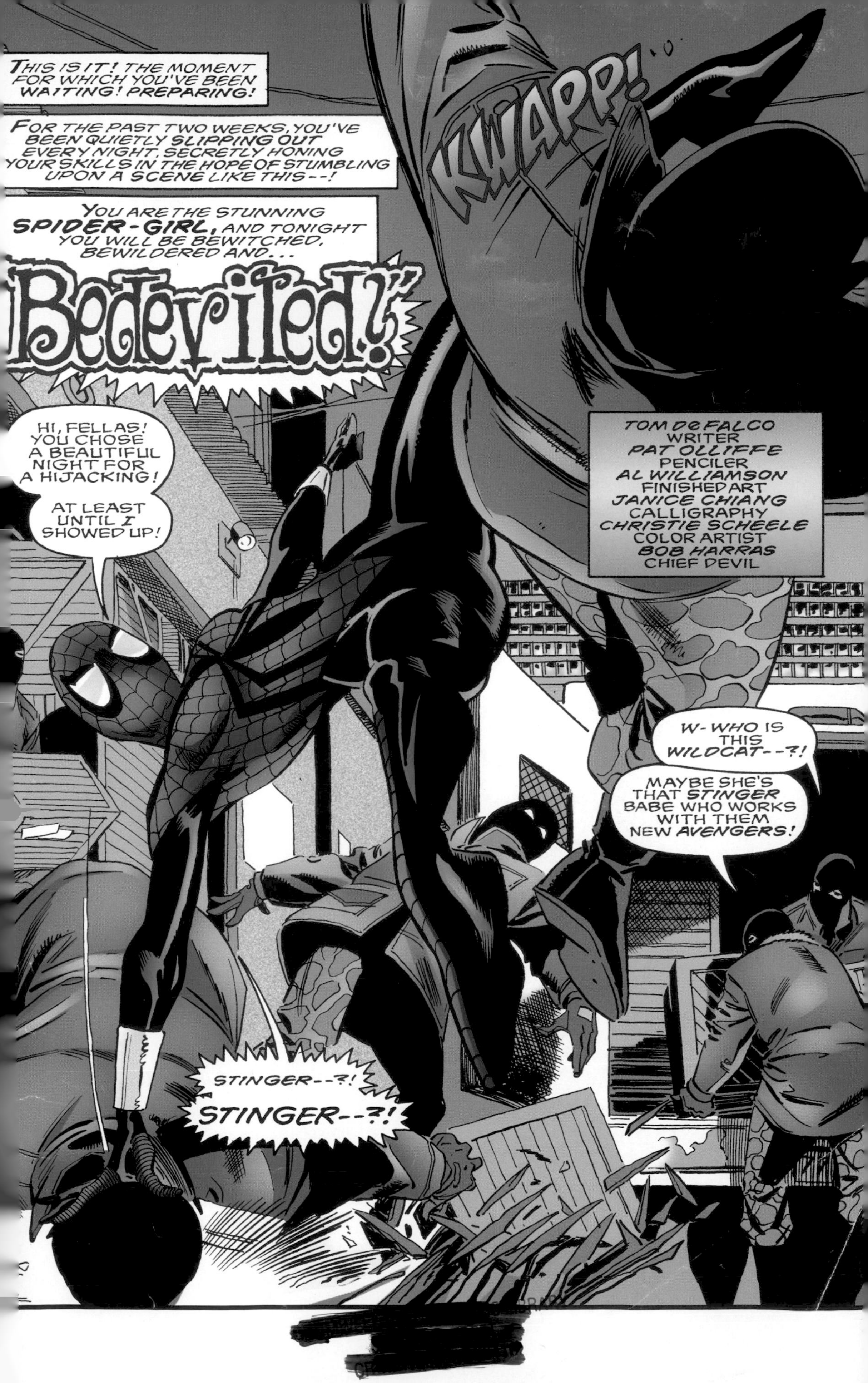
KWAPP!
THIS IS IT! THE MOMENT FOR WHICH YOU'VE BEEN WAITING! PREPARING!
FOR THE PAST TWO WEEKS, YOU'VE BEEN QUIETLY SLIPPING OUT EVERY NIGHT, SECRETLY HONING YOUR SKILLS IN THE HOPE OF STUMBLING UPON A SCENE LIKE THIS--!
YOU ARE THE STUNNING SPIDER-GIRL, AND TONIGHT YOU WILL BE BEWITCHED, BEWILDERED AND...
"Bedeviled!?"
HI, FELLAS! YOU CHOSE A BEAUTIFUL NIGHT FOR A HIJACKING!
AT LEAST UNTIL I SHOWED UP!
TOM DeFALCO WRITER
PAT OLLIFFE PENCILER
AL WILLIAMSON FINISHED ART
JANICE CHIANG CALLIGRAPHY
CHRISTIE SCHEELE COLOR ARTIST
BOB HARRAS CHIEF DEVIL
W-WHO IS THIS WILDCAT--?!
MAYBE SHE'S THAT STINGER BABE WHO WORKS WITH THEM NEW AVENGERS!
STINGER--?!
STINGER--?!

[redacted]

VISIT US AT

www.abdopub.com

Spotlight, a division of ABDO Publishing Company Inc., is the school and library distributor of the Marvel Entertainment books.

Library bound edition © 2006

Library of Congress Cataloging-in-Publication Data

Bedeviled!

ISBN 1-59961-027-2 (Reinforced Library Bound Edition)

All Spotlight books are reinforced library binding
and manufactured in the United States of America

Spotlight

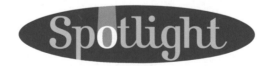

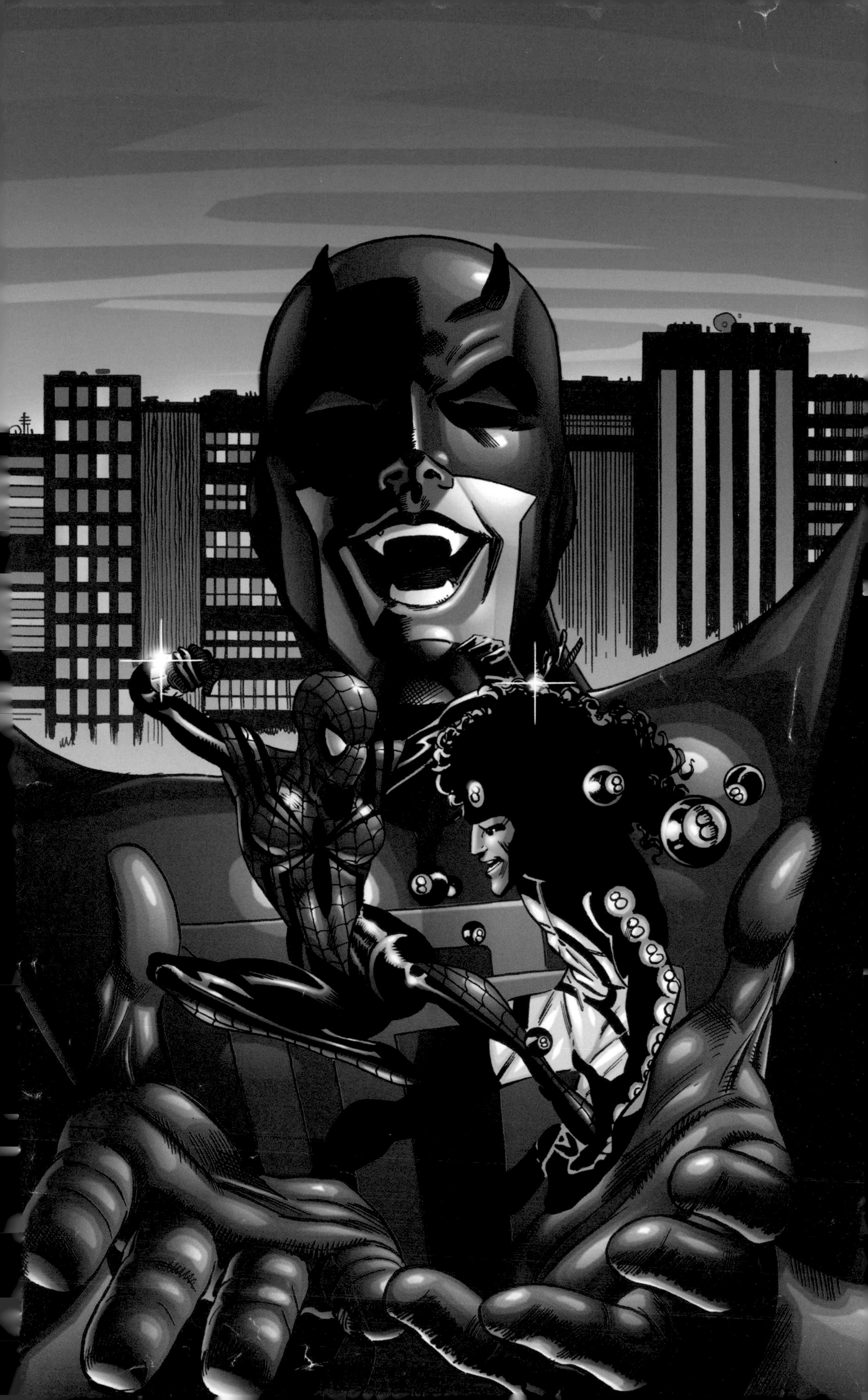

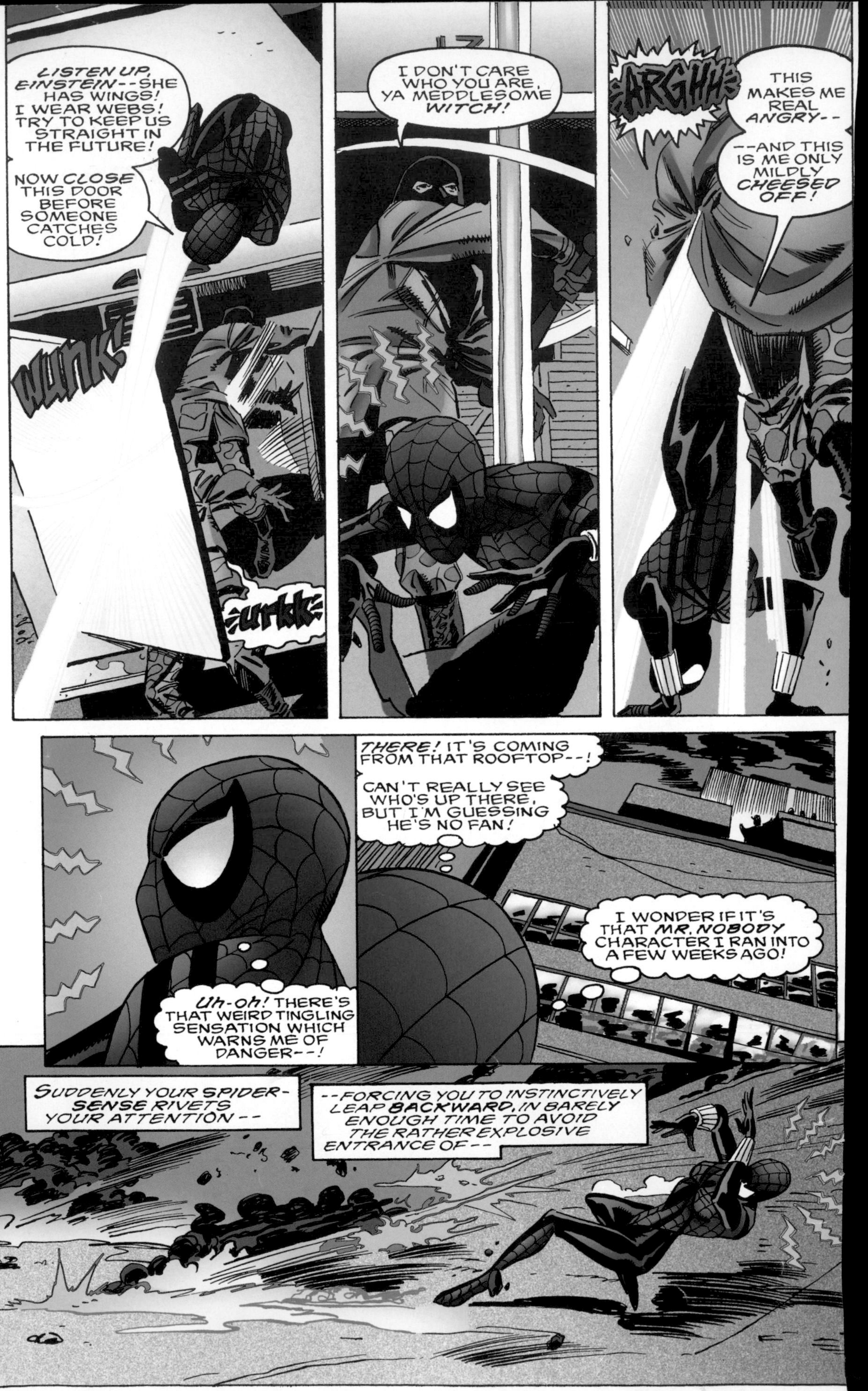

LISTEN UP, EINSTEIN--SHE HAS WINGS! I WEAR WEBS! TRY TO KEEP US STRAIGHT IN THE FUTURE!
NOW CLOSE THIS DOOR BEFORE SOMEONE CATCHES COLD!
WUNK!
URKK
I DON'T CARE WHO YOU ARE, YA MEDDLESOME WITCH!
ARGHH
THIS MAKES ME REAL ANGRY--
--AND THIS IS ME ONLY MILDLY CHEESED OFF!
Uh-oh! THERE'S THAT WEIRD TINGLING SENSATION WHICH WARNS ME OF DANGER--!
THERE! IT'S COMING FROM THAT ROOFTOP--!
CAN'T REALLY SEE WHO'S UP THERE, BUT I'M GUESSING HE'S NO FAN!
I WONDER IF IT'S THAT MR. NOBODY CHARACTER I RAN INTO A FEW WEEKS AGO!
SUDDENLY YOUR SPIDER-SENSE RIVETS YOUR ATTENTION--
--FORCING YOU TO INSTINCTIVELY LEAP BACKWARD, IN BARELY ENOUGH TIME TO AVOID THE RATHER EXPLOSIVE ENTRANCE OF--

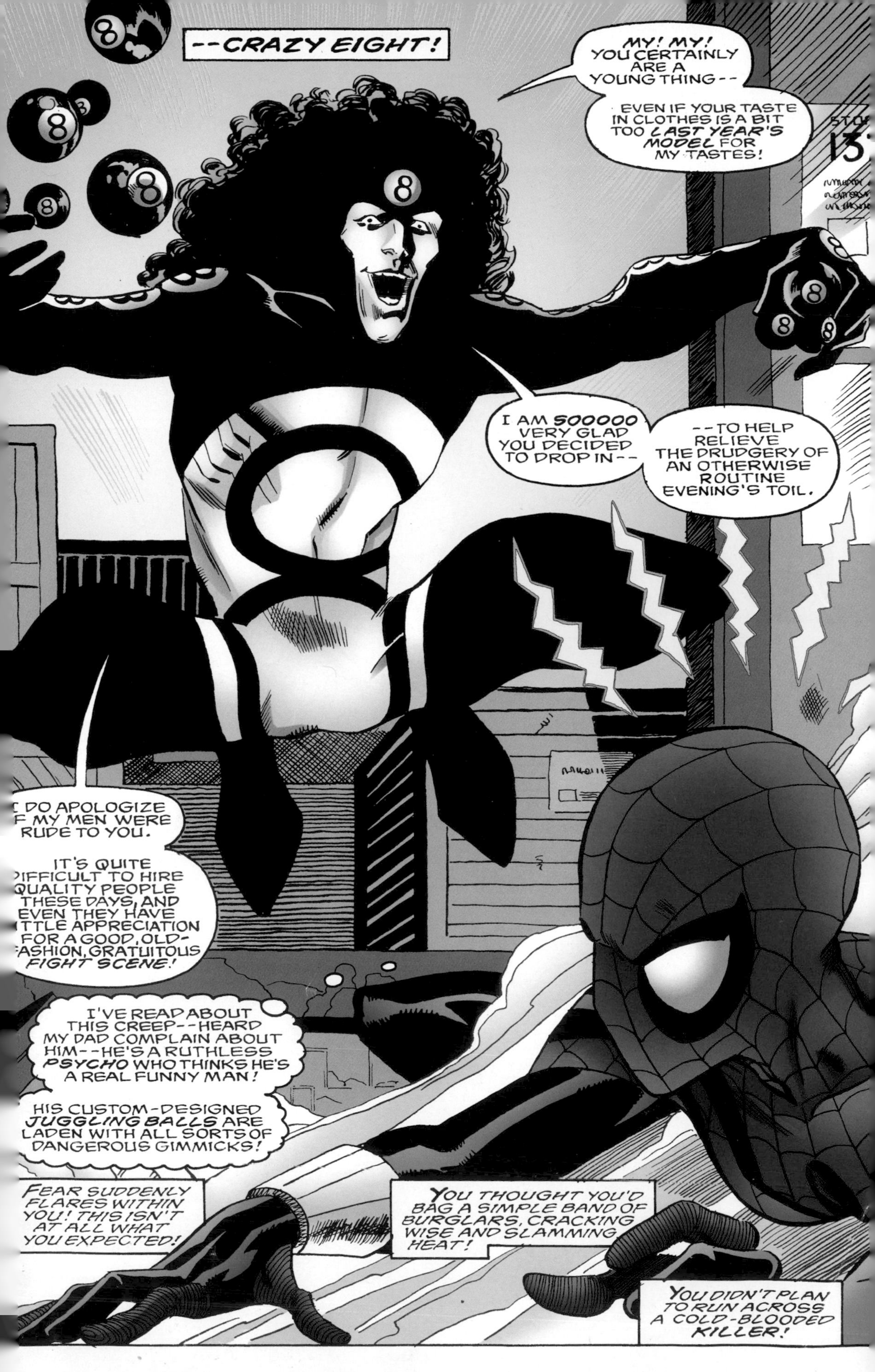
--CRAZY EIGHT!
MY! MY! YOU CERTAINLY ARE A YOUNG THING--
EVEN IF YOUR TASTE IN CLOTHES IS A BIT TOO LAST YEAR'S MODEL FOR MY TASTES!
I AM SOOOOO VERY GLAD YOU DECIDED TO DROP IN--
--TO HELP RELIEVE THE DRUDGERY OF AN OTHERWISE ROUTINE EVENING'S TOIL.
I DO APOLOGIZE IF MY MEN WERE RUDE TO YOU.
IT'S QUITE DIFFICULT TO HIRE QUALITY PEOPLE THESE DAYS, AND EVEN THEY HAVE LITTLE APPRECIATION FOR A GOOD, OLD-FASHION, GRATUITOUS FIGHT SCENE!
I'VE READ ABOUT THIS CREEP--HEARD MY DAD COMPLAIN ABOUT HIM--HE'S A RUTHLESS PSYCHO WHO THINKS HE'S A REAL FUNNY MAN!
HIS CUSTOM-DESIGNED JUGGLING BALLS ARE LADEN WITH ALL SORTS OF DANGEROUS GIMMICKS!
FEAR SUDDENLY FLARES WITHIN YOU! THIS ISN'T AT ALL WHAT YOU EXPECTED!
YOU THOUGHT YOU'D BAG A SIMPLE BAND OF BURGLARS, CRACKING WISE AND SLAMMING HEAT!
YOU DIDN'T PLAN TO RUN ACROSS A COLD-BLOODED KILLER!

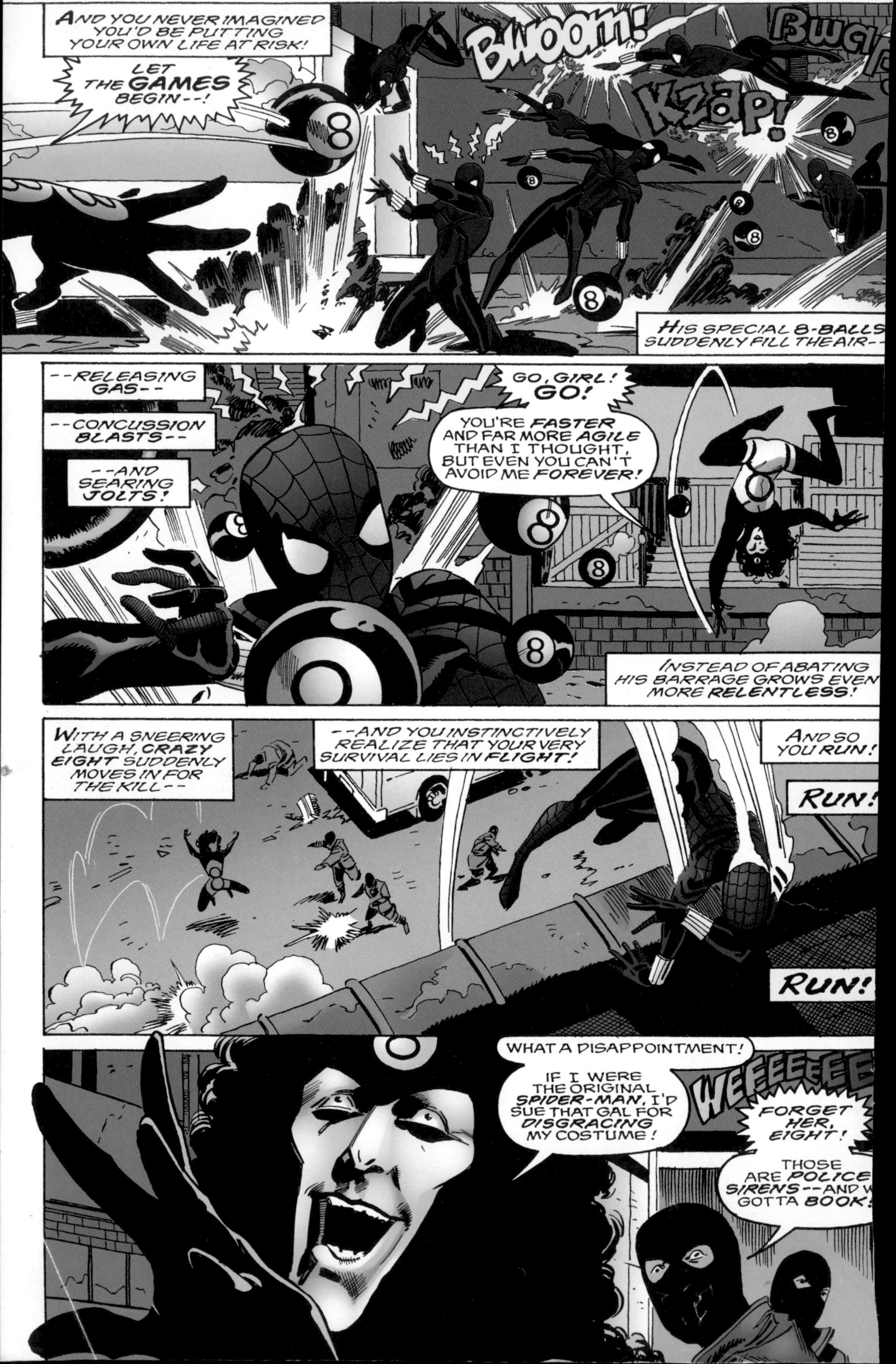
AND YOU NEVER IMAGINED YOU'D BE PUTTING YOUR OWN LIFE AT RISK!
LET THE GAMES BEGIN--!
BWOOM!
KZAP!
HIS SPECIAL 8-BALLS SUDDENLY FILL THE AIR--
--RELEASING GAS--
--CONCUSSION BLASTS--
--AND SEARING JOLTS!
GO, GIRL! GO!
YOU'RE FASTER AND FAR MORE AGILE THAN I THOUGHT, BUT EVEN YOU CAN'T AVOID ME FOREVER!
INSTEAD OF ABATING HIS BARRAGE GROWS EVEN MORE RELENTLESS!
WITH A SNEERING LAUGH, CRAZY EIGHT SUDDENLY MOVES IN FOR THE KILL--
--AND YOU INSTINCTIVELY REALIZE THAT YOUR VERY SURVIVAL LIES IN FLIGHT!
AND SO YOU RUN!
RUN!
RUN!
WHAT A DISAPPOINTMENT!
IF I WERE THE ORIGINAL SPIDER-MAN, I'D SUE THAT GAL FOR DISGRACING MY COSTUME!
FORGET HER, EIGHT!
THOSE ARE POLICE SIRENS--AND W GOTTA BOOK!

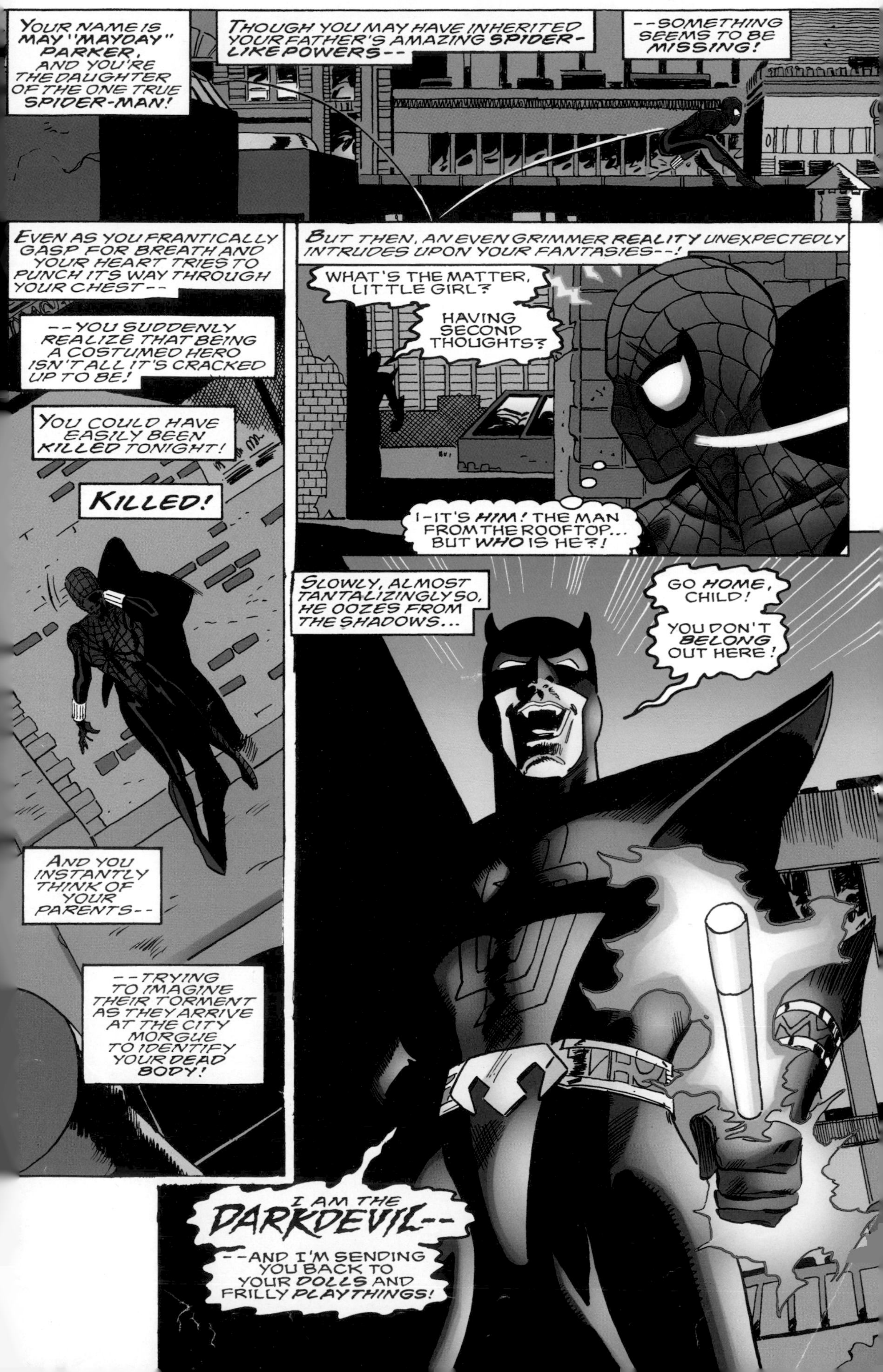
YOUR NAME IS MAY "MAYDAY" PARKER, AND YOU'RE THE DAUGHTER OF THE ONE TRUE SPIDER-MAN!
THOUGH YOU MAY HAVE INHERITED YOUR FATHER'S AMAZING SPIDER-LIKE POWERS--
--SOMETHING SEEMS TO BE MISSING!
EVEN AS YOU FRANTICALLY GASP FOR BREATH AND YOUR HEART TRIES TO PUNCH IT'S WAY THROUGH YOUR CHEST--
--YOU SUDDENLY REALIZE THAT BEING A COSTUMED HERO ISN'T ALL IT'S CRACKED UP TO BE!
YOU COULD HAVE EASILY BEEN KILLED TONIGHT!
KILLED!
AND YOU INSTANTLY THINK OF YOUR PARENTS--
--TRYING TO IMAGINE THEIR TORMENT AS THEY ARRIVE AT THE CITY MORGUE TO IDENTIFY YOUR DEAD BODY!
BUT THEN, AN EVEN GRIMMER REALITY UNEXPECTEDLY INTRUDES UPON YOUR FANTASIES--!
WHAT'S THE MATTER, LITTLE GIRL?
HAVING SECOND THOUGHTS?
I-IT'S HIM! THE MAN FROM THE ROOFTOP... BUT WHO IS HE?!
SLOWLY, ALMOST TANTALIZINGLY SO, HE OOZES FROM THE SHADOWS...
GO HOME, CHILD!
YOU DON'T BELONG OUT HERE!
I AM THE DARKDEVIL--
--AND I'M SENDING YOU BACK TO YOUR DOLLS AND FRILLY PLAYTHINGS!

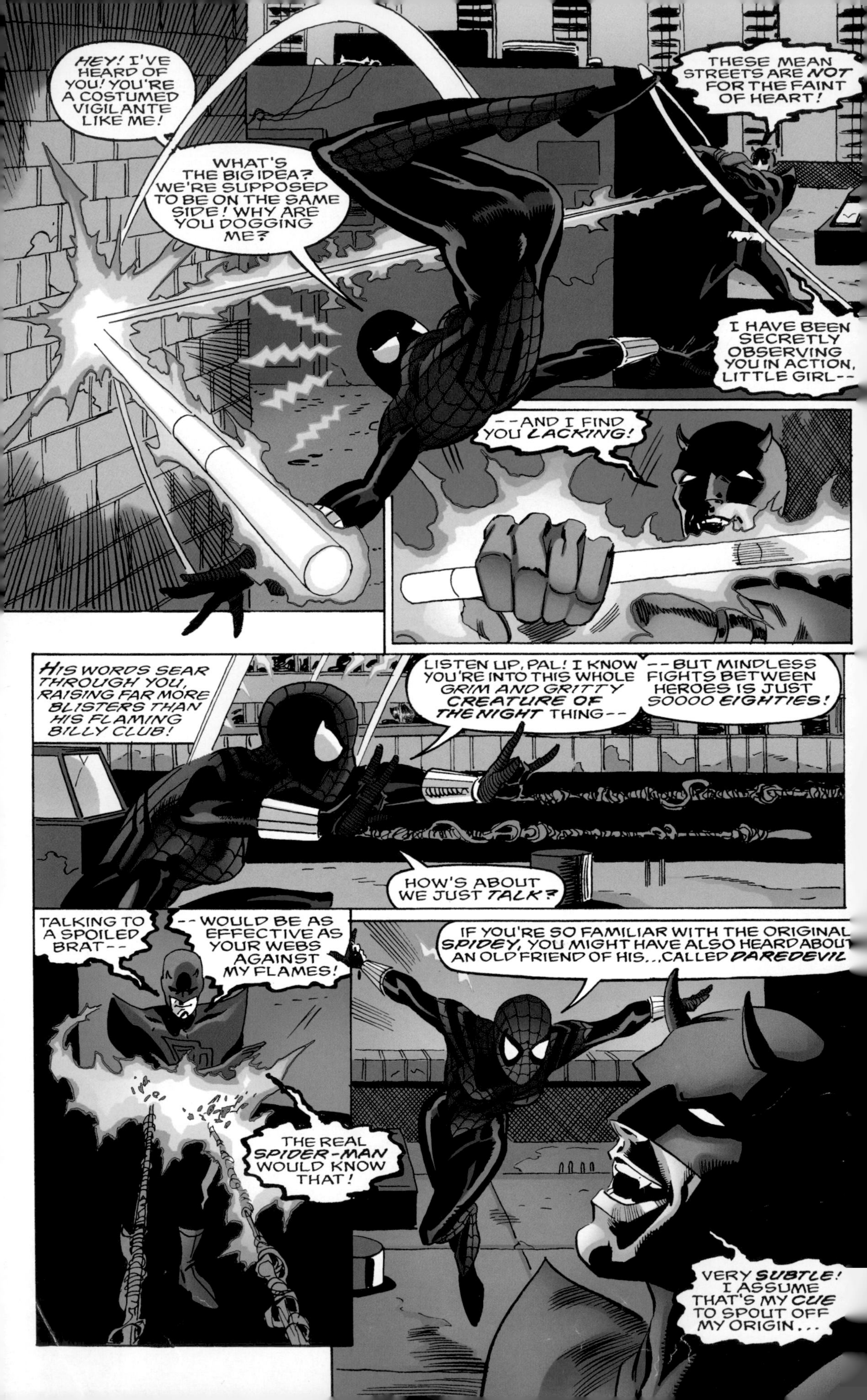
HEY! I'VE HEARD OF YOU! YOU'RE A COSTUMED VIGILANTE LIKE ME!
WHAT'S THE BIG IDEA? WE'RE SUPPOSED TO BE ON THE SAME SIDE! WHY ARE YOU DOGGING ME?
THESE MEAN STREETS ARE NOT FOR THE FAINT OF HEART!
I HAVE BEEN SECRETLY OBSERVING YOU IN ACTION, LITTLE GIRL--
--AND I FIND YOU LACKING!
HIS WORDS SEAR THROUGH YOU, RAISING FAR MORE BLISTERS THAN HIS FLAMING BILLY CLUB!
LISTEN UP, PAL! I KNOW YOU'RE INTO THIS WHOLE GRIM AND GRITTY CREATURE OF THE NIGHT THING--
--BUT MINDLESS FIGHTS BETWEEN HEROES IS JUST SOOOO EIGHTIES!
HOW'S ABOUT WE JUST TALK?
TALKING TO A SPOILED BRAT--
--WOULD BE AS EFFECTIVE AS YOUR WEBS AGAINST MY FLAMES!
THE REAL SPIDER-MAN WOULD KNOW THAT!
IF YOU'RE SO FAMILIAR WITH THE ORIGINAL SPIDEY, YOU MIGHT HAVE ALSO HEARD ABOUT AN OLD FRIEND OF HIS...CALLED DAREDEVIL
VERY SUBTLE! I ASSUME THAT'S MY CUE TO SPOUT OFF MY ORIGIN...

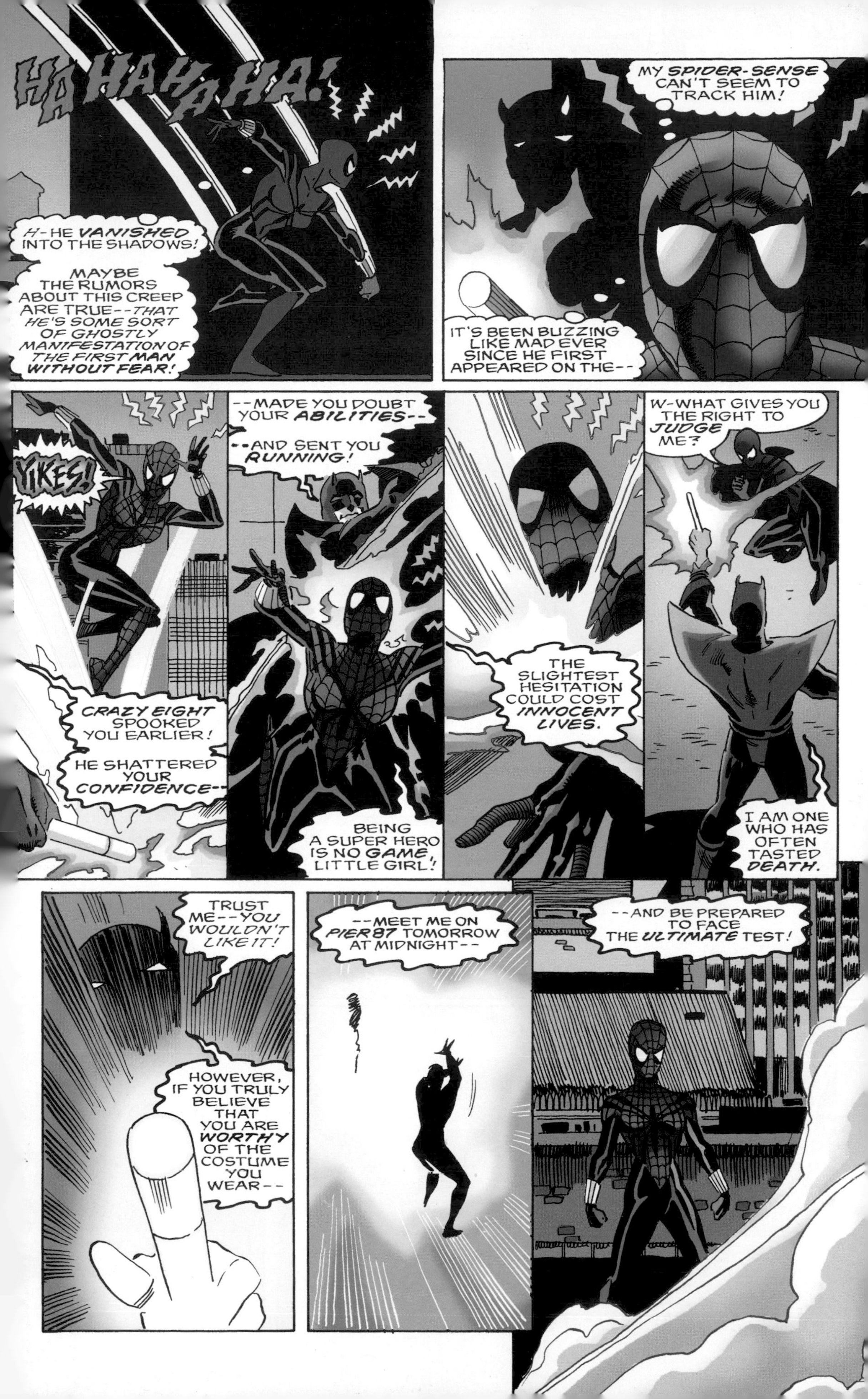
HA HA HA HA HA!
H-HE VANISHED INTO THE SHADOWS!
MAYBE THE RUMORS ABOUT THIS CREEP ARE TRUE--THAT HE'S SOME SORT OF GHOSTLY MANIFESTATION OF THE FIRST MAN WITHOUT FEAR!
MY SPIDER-SENSE CAN'T SEEM TO TRACK HIM!
IT'S BEEN BUZZING LIKE MAD EVER SINCE HE FIRST APPEARED ON THE--
YIKES!
CRAZY EIGHT SPOOKED YOU EARLIER!
HE SHATTERED YOUR CONFIDENCE--
--MADE YOU DOUBT YOUR ABILITIES--
--AND SENT YOU RUNNING!
BEING A SUPER HERO IS NO GAME, LITTLE GIRL!
THE SLIGHTEST HESITATION COULD COST INNOCENT LIVES.
W-WHAT GIVES YOU THE RIGHT TO JUDGE ME?
I AM ONE WHO HAS OFTEN TASTED DEATH.
TRUST ME--YOU WOULDN'T LIKE IT!
HOWEVER, IF YOU TRULY BELIEVE THAT YOU ARE WORTHY OF THE COSTUME YOU WEAR--
--MEET ME ON PIER 87 TOMORROW AT MIDNIGHT--
--AND BE PREPARED TO FACE THE ULTIMATE TEST!

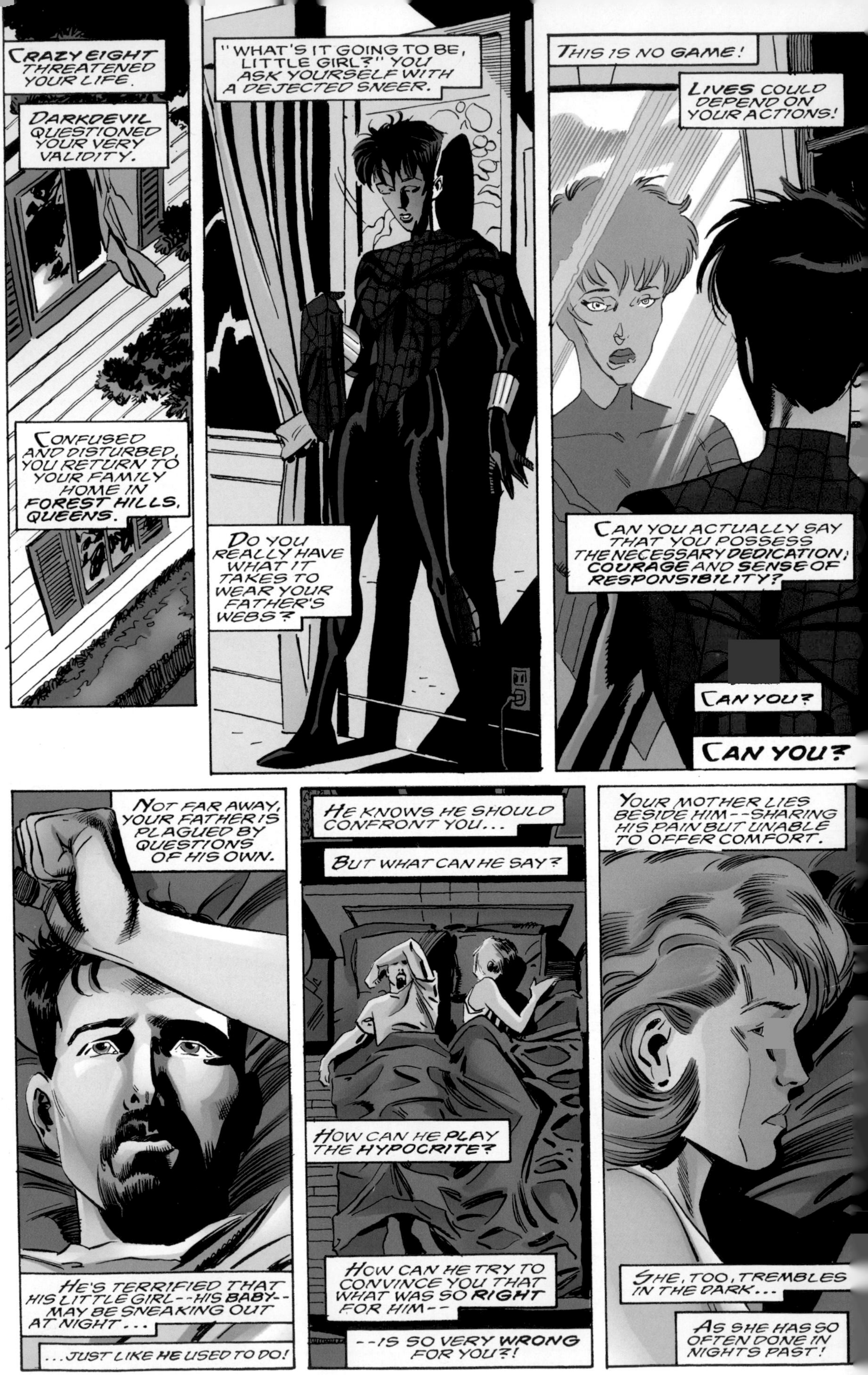
CRAZY EIGHT THREATENED YOUR LIFE.
DARKDEVIL QUESTIONED YOUR VERY VALIDITY.
CONFUSED AND DISTURBED, YOU RETURN TO YOUR FAMILY HOME IN FOREST HILLS, QUEENS.
"WHAT'S IT GOING TO BE, LITTLE GIRL?" YOU ASK YOURSELF WITH A DEJECTED SNEER.
DO YOU REALLY HAVE WHAT IT TAKES TO WEAR YOUR FATHER'S WEBS?
THIS IS NO GAME!
LIVES COULD DEPEND ON YOUR ACTIONS!
CAN YOU ACTUALLY SAY THAT YOU POSSESS THE NECESSARY DEDICATION; COURAGE AND SENSE OF RESPONSIBILITY?
CAN YOU?
CAN YOU?
NOT FAR AWAY, YOUR FATHER IS PLAGUED BY QUESTIONS OF HIS OWN.
HE'S TERRIFIED THAT HIS LITTLE GIRL--HIS BABY--MAY BE SNEAKING OUT AT NIGHT...
...JUST LIKE HE USED TO DO!
HE KNOWS HE SHOULD CONFRONT YOU...
BUT WHAT CAN HE SAY?
HOW CAN HE PLAY THE HYPOCRITE?
HOW CAN HE TRY TO CONVINCE YOU THAT WHAT WAS SO RIGHT FOR HIM--
--IS SO VERY WRONG FOR YOU?!
YOUR MOTHER LIES BESIDE HIM--SHARING HIS PAIN BUT UNABLE TO OFFER COMFORT.
SHE, TOO, TREMBLES IN THE DARK...
AS SHE HAS SO OFTEN DONE IN NIGHTS PAST!

EARLY THE NEXT MORNING, YOU CHANCE TO OVERHEAR A CONVERSATION NOT MEANT FOR YOUR EARS...

WE CAN'T GO ON LIKE THIS, PETER. YOU HAVE TO *TALK* TO YOUR DAUGHTER.

I... I KNOW, MARY JANE.

I'M SORRY I PUT IT OFF SO LONG, BUT... WELL... MAY AND I ARE SUPPOSED TO HAVE *LUNCH* TODAY.

YOU'LL FEEL *BETTER* ONCE EVERYTHING'S OUT IN THE OPEN.

YOU DRAG TO SCHOOL WITH A NEW WEIGHT ON YOUR SHOULDERS.

DTOWN HIGH SCHOOL

YOU USED TO LOOK FORWARD TO LUNCH WITH DAD!

HE'D DISCUSS HIS WORK IN THE *POLICE LAB,* AND YOU'D RAMBLE ON ABOUT *SCHOOL, SPORTS* AND *WHATEVER!*

BUT THAT WAS BEFORE YOUR LIFE BLOSSOMED WITH SECRETS!

YO, MAY--! WHERE HAVE YOU BEEN?

I EXPECTED TO SEE YOU AT THE *LIBRARY* LAST NIGHT.

SORRY, JIMMY! SOMETHING... *UNEXPECTED* POPPED UP!

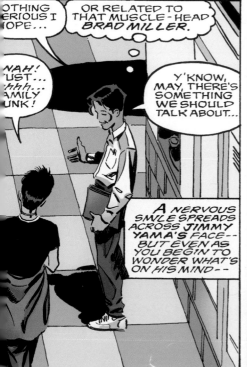

OTHING ERIOUS I HOPE...

OR RELATED TO THAT MUSCLE-HEAD *BRAD MILLER.*

NAH! UST... HHH... AMILY UNK!

Y'KNOW, MAY, THERE'S SOMETHING WE SHOULD TALK ABOUT...

A NERVOUS SMILE SPREADS ACROSS *JIMMY YAMA'S* FACE-- BUT EVEN AS YOU BEGIN TO WONDER WHAT'S ON HIS MIND--

--A FAMILIAR TINGLING SUDDENLY WARNS YOU TO FREEZE IN PLACE--

--AND YOU INSTANTLY SEE HOW EVERYONE COULD BENEFIT FROM A *SPIDER-SENSE!*

PWAM!

ufft

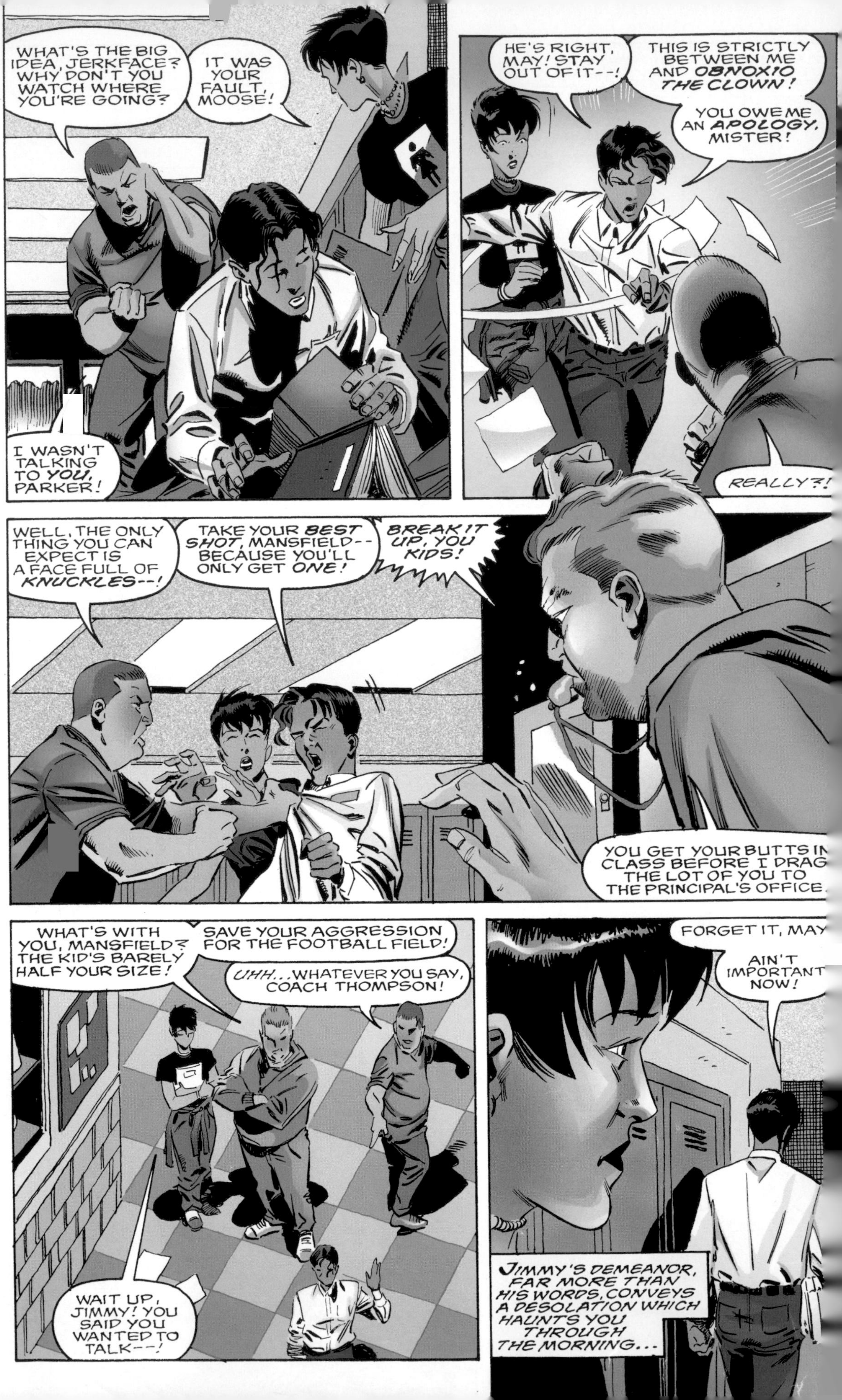
WHAT'S THE BIG IDEA, JERKFACE? WHY DON'T YOU WATCH WHERE YOU'RE GOING?
IT WAS YOUR FAULT, MOOSE!
I WASN'T TALKING TO YOU, PARKER!
HE'S RIGHT, MAY! STAY OUT OF IT--!
THIS IS STRICTLY BETWEEN ME AND OBNOXIO THE CLOWN!
YOU OWE ME AN APOLOGY, MISTER!
REALLY?!
WELL, THE ONLY THING YOU CAN EXPECT IS A FACE FULL OF KNUCKLES--!
TAKE YOUR BEST SHOT, MANSFIELD-- BECAUSE YOU'LL ONLY GET ONE!
BREAK IT UP, YOU KIDS!
YOU GET YOUR BUTTS IN CLASS BEFORE I DRAG THE LOT OF YOU TO THE PRINCIPAL'S OFFICE.
WHAT'S WITH YOU, MANSFIELD? THE KID'S BARELY HALF YOUR SIZE!
SAVE YOUR AGGRESSION FOR THE FOOTBALL FIELD!
UHH... WHATEVER YOU SAY, COACH THOMPSON!
WAIT UP, JIMMY! YOU SAID YOU WANTED TO TALK--!
FORGET IT, MAY
AIN'T IMPORTANT NOW!
JIMMY'S DEMEANOR, FAR MORE THAN HIS WORDS, CONVEYS A DESOLATION WHICH HAUNTS YOU THROUGH THE MORNING...

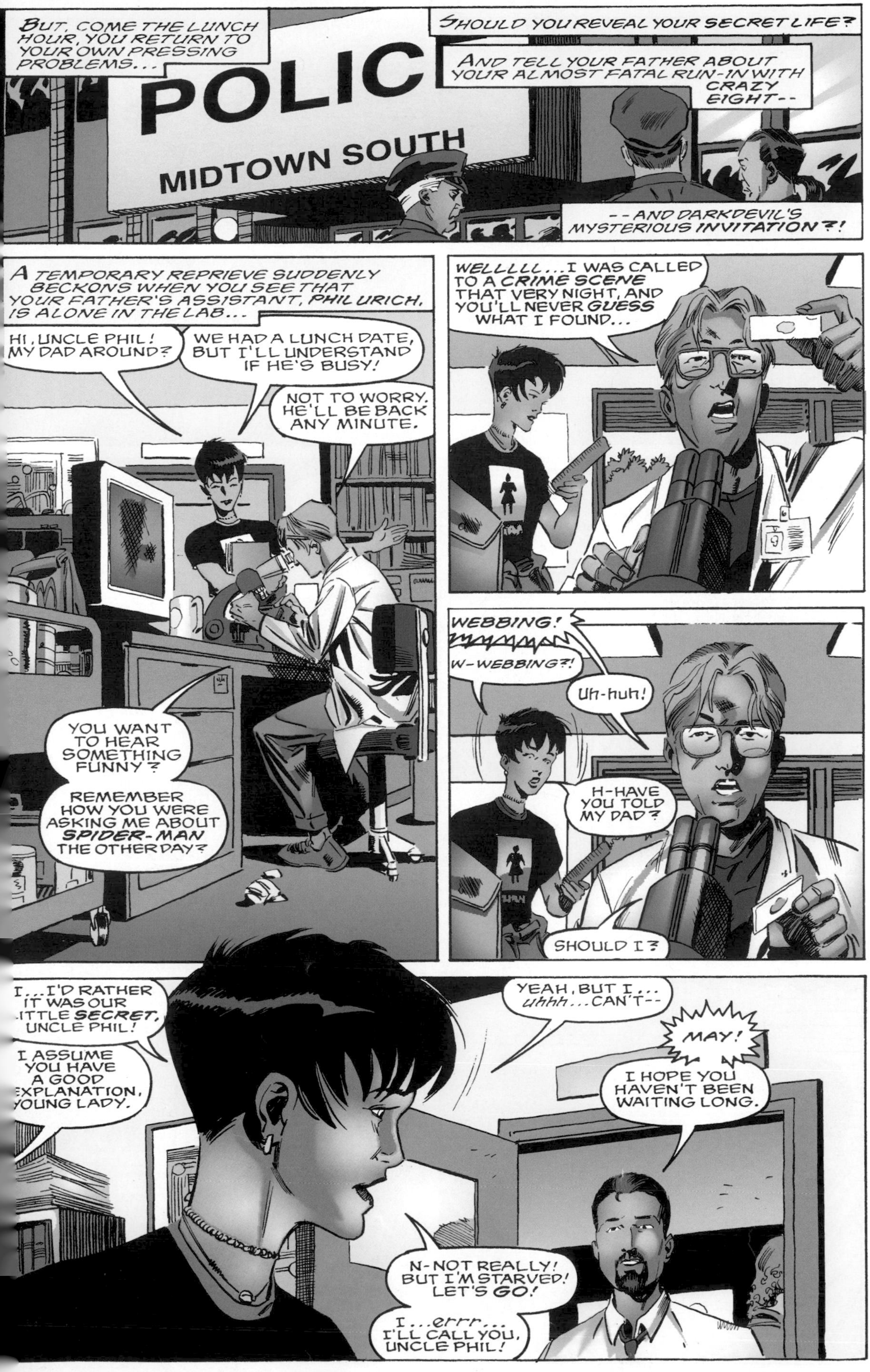

BUT, COME THE LUNCH HOUR, YOU RETURN TO YOUR OWN PRESSING PROBLEMS...
POLIC
MIDTOWN SOUTH
SHOULD YOU REVEAL YOUR SECRET LIFE?
AND TELL YOUR FATHER ABOUT YOUR ALMOST FATAL RUN-IN WITH CRAZY EIGHT--
--AND DARKDEVIL'S MYSTERIOUS INVITATION?!
A TEMPORARY REPRIEVE SUDDENLY BECKONS WHEN YOU SEE THAT YOUR FATHER'S ASSISTANT, PHIL URICH, IS ALONE IN THE LAB...
HI, UNCLE PHIL! MY DAD AROUND?
WE HAD A LUNCH DATE, BUT I'LL UNDERSTAND IF HE'S BUSY!
NOT TO WORRY. HE'LL BE BACK ANY MINUTE.
YOU WANT TO HEAR SOMETHING FUNNY?
REMEMBER HOW YOU WERE ASKING ME ABOUT SPIDER-MAN THE OTHER DAY?
WELLLLL...I WAS CALLED TO A CRIME SCENE THAT VERY NIGHT, AND YOU'LL NEVER GUESS WHAT I FOUND...
WEBBING!
W-WEBBING?!
Uh-huh!
H-HAVE YOU TOLD MY DAD?
SHOULD I?
I...I'D RATHER IT WAS OUR LITTLE SECRET, UNCLE PHIL!
I ASSUME YOU HAVE A GOOD EXPLANATION, YOUNG LADY.
YEAH, BUT I... uhhh...CAN'T--
MAY!
I HOPE YOU HAVEN'T BEEN WAITING LONG.
N-NOT REALLY! BUT I'M STARVED! LET'S GO!
I...errr... I'LL CALL YOU, UNCLE PHIL!

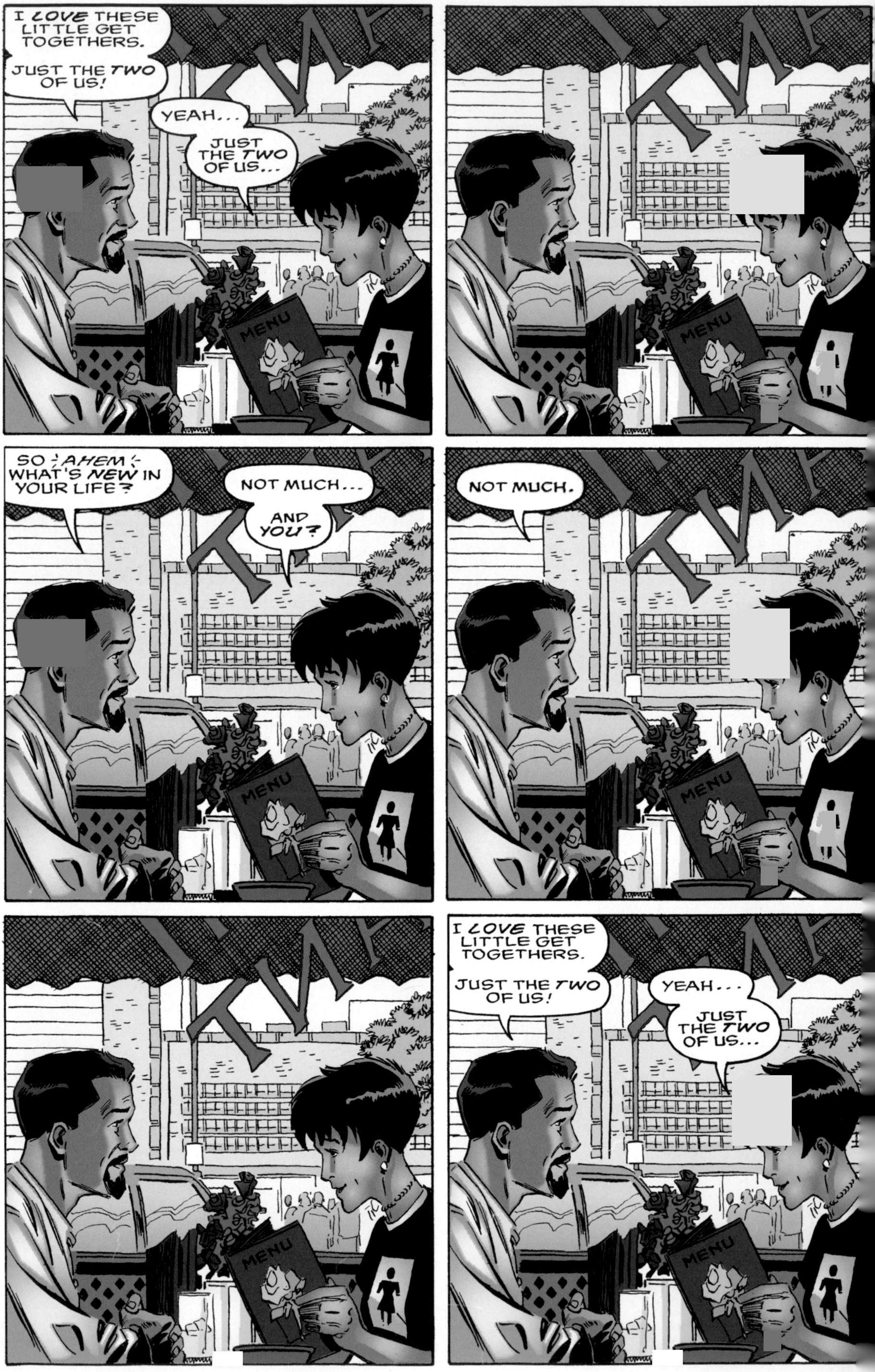
I LOVE THESE LITTLE GET TOGETHERS.
JUST THE TWO OF US!
YEAH...
JUST THE TWO OF US...
SO ;AHEM; WHAT'S NEW IN YOUR LIFE?
NOT MUCH...
AND YOU?
NOT MUCH.
I LOVE THESE LITTLE GET TOGETHERS.
JUST THE TWO OF US!
YEAH...
JUST THE TWO OF US...

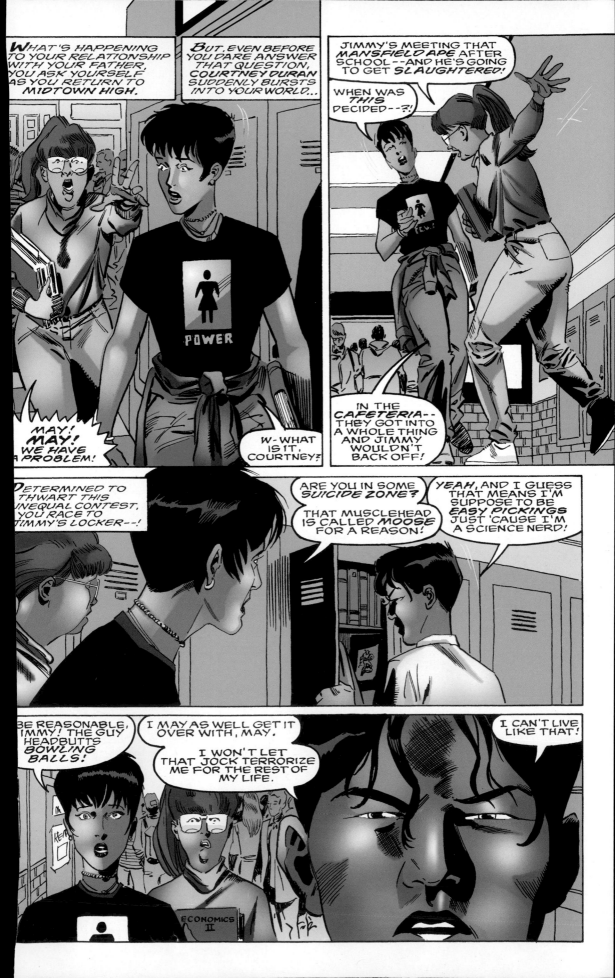

WHAT'S HAPPENING TO YOUR RELATIONSHIP WITH YOUR FATHER, YOU ASK YOURSELF AS YOU RETURN TO MIDTOWN HIGH.

BUT, EVEN BEFORE YOU DARE ANSWER THAT QUESTION, COURTNEY DURAN SUDDENLY BURSTS INTO YOUR WORLD...

JIMMY'S MEETING THAT *MANSFIELD APE* AFTER SCHOOL--AND HE'S GOING TO GET *SLAUGHTERED!*

WHEN WAS *THIS* DECIDED--?!

MAY! *MAY!* WE HAVE A *PROBLEM!*

W-WHAT IS IT, COURTNEY?

IN THE *CAFETERIA*--THEY GOT INTO A WHOLE THING AND JIMMY WOULDN'T BACK OFF!

POWER

DETERMINED TO THWART THIS UNEQUAL CONTEST, YOU RACE TO JIMMY'S LOCKER--!

ARE YOU IN SOME *SUICIDE ZONE?* THAT MUSCLEHEAD IS CALLED *MOOSE* FOR A REASON!

YEAH, AND I GUESS THAT MEANS I'M SUPPOSE TO BE *EASY PICKINGS* JUST 'CAUSE I'M A SCIENCE NERD!

BE REASONABLE, JIMMY! THE GUY HEADBUTTS BOWLING BALLS!

I MAY AS WELL GET IT OVER WITH, MAY.

I WON'T LET THAT JOCK TERRORIZE ME FOR THE REST OF MY LIFE.

I CAN'T LIVE LIKE THAT!

ECONOMICS II

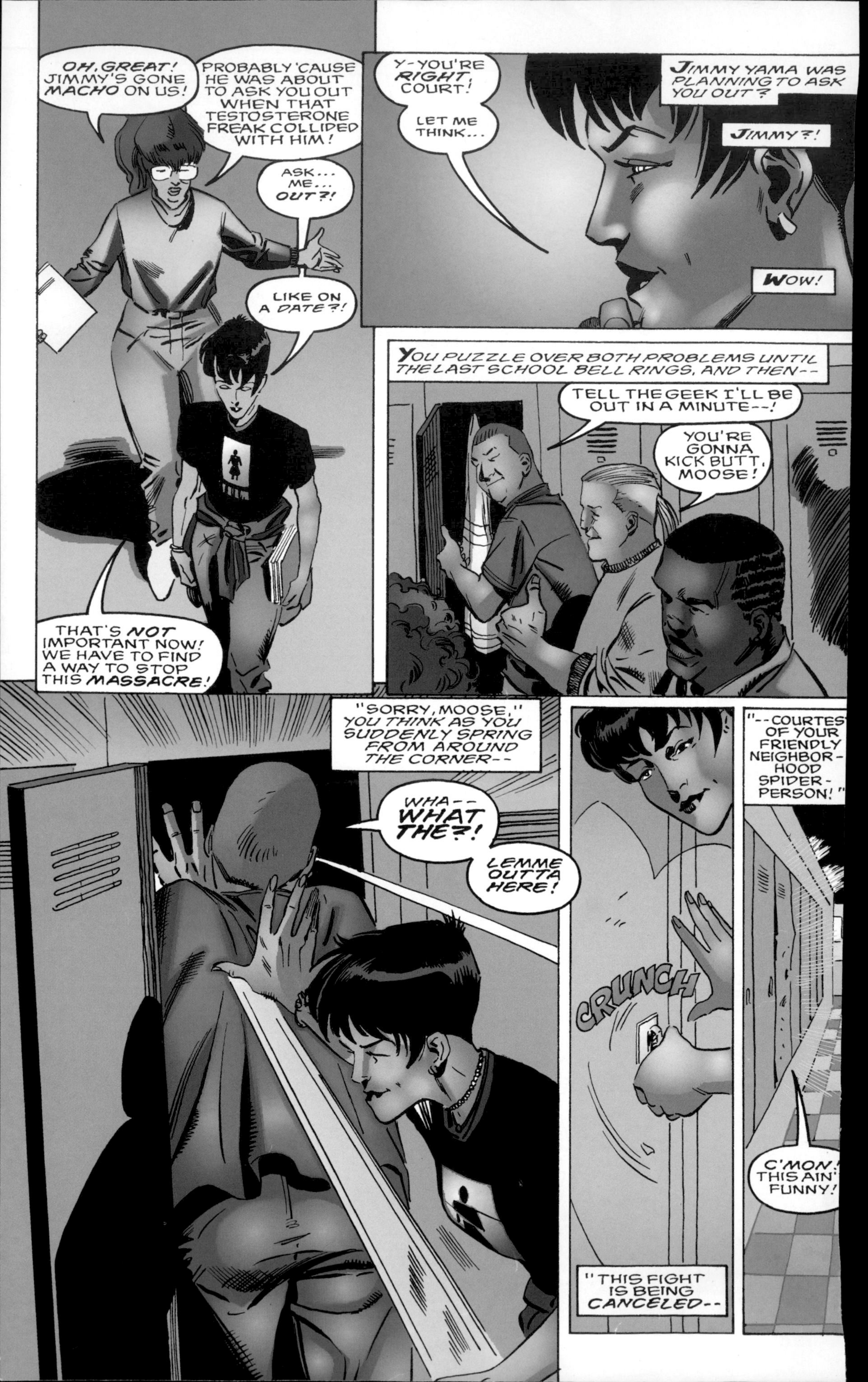
OH, GREAT! JIMMY'S GONE MACHO ON US!
PROBABLY 'CAUSE HE WAS ABOUT TO ASK YOU OUT WHEN THAT TESTOSTERONE FREAK COLLIDED WITH HIM!
ASK... ME... OUT?!
LIKE ON A DATE?!
THAT'S NOT IMPORTANT NOW! WE HAVE TO FIND A WAY TO STOP THIS MASSACRE!
Y-YOU'RE RIGHT, COURT!
LET ME THINK...
JIMMY YAMA WAS PLANNING TO ASK YOU OUT?
JIMMY?!
WOW!
YOU PUZZLE OVER BOTH PROBLEMS UNTIL THE LAST SCHOOL BELL RINGS, AND THEN--
TELL THE GEEK I'LL BE OUT IN A MINUTE--!
YOU'RE GONNA KICK BUTT, MOOSE!
"SORRY, MOOSE," YOU THINK AS YOU SUDDENLY SPRING FROM AROUND THE CORNER--
WHA-- WHAT THE?!
LEMME OUTTA HERE!
"THIS FIGHT IS BEING CANCELED--
CRUNCH
"--COURTES OF YOUR FRIENDLY NEIGHBOR-HOOD SPIDER-PERSON!"
C'MON! THIS AIN' FUNNY!

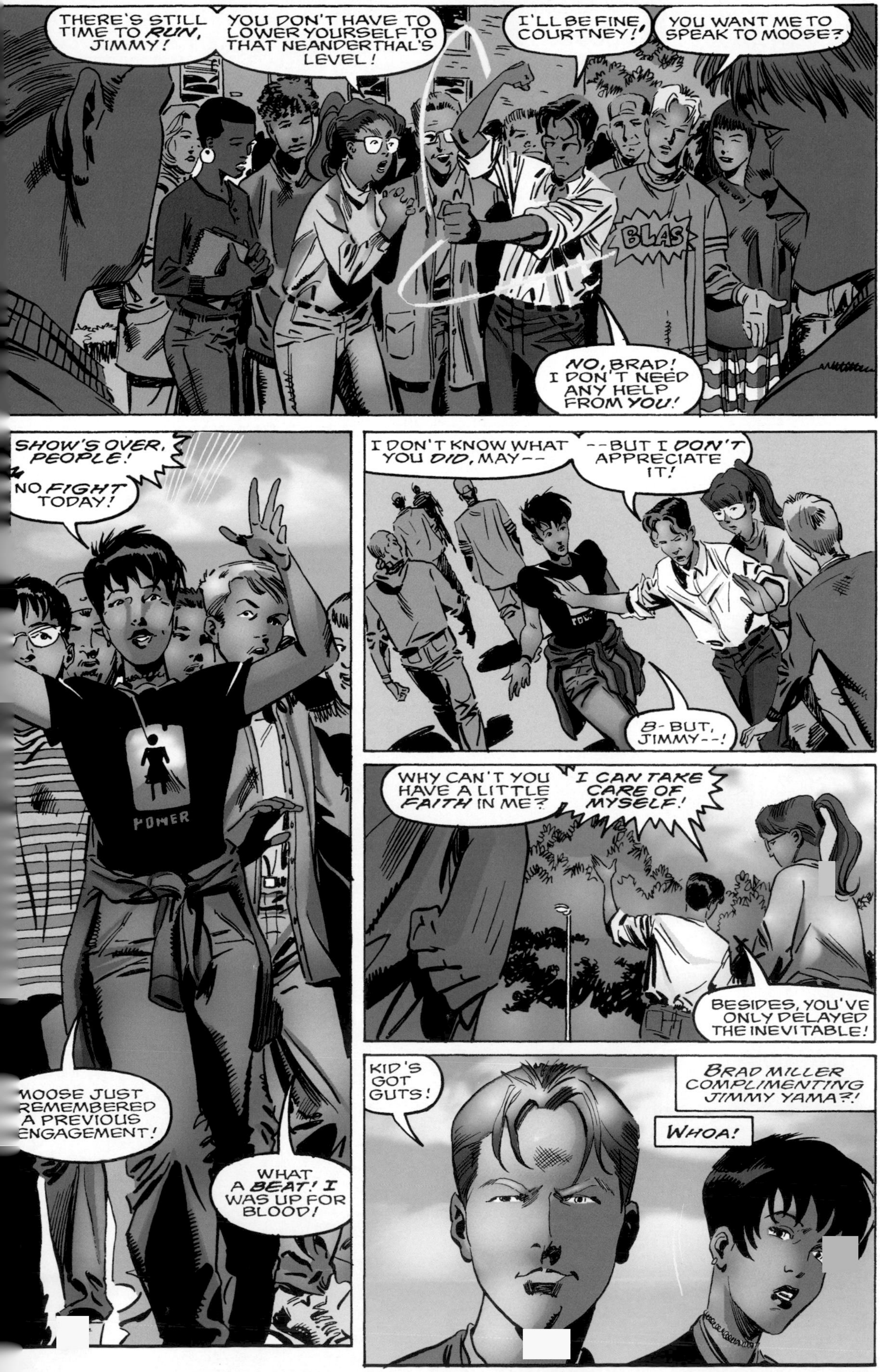
THERE'S STILL TIME TO RUN, JIMMY!
YOU DON'T HAVE TO LOWER YOURSELF TO THAT NEANDERTHAL'S LEVEL!
I'LL BE FINE, COURTNEY!
YOU WANT ME TO SPEAK TO MOOSE?
BLAS
NO, BRAD! I DON'T NEED ANY HELP FROM YOU!
SHOW'S OVER, PEOPLE!
NO FIGHT TODAY!
POWER
MOOSE JUST REMEMBERED A PREVIOUS ENGAGEMENT!
WHAT A BEAT! I WAS UP FOR BLOOD!
I DON'T KNOW WHAT YOU DID, MAY--
--BUT I DON'T APPRECIATE IT!
B-BUT, JIMMY--!
WHY CAN'T YOU HAVE A LITTLE FAITH IN ME?
I CAN TAKE CARE OF MYSELF!
BESIDES, YOU'VE ONLY DELAYED THE INEVITABLE!
KID'S GOT GUTS!
BRAD MILLER COMPLIMENTING JIMMY YAMA?!
WHOA!

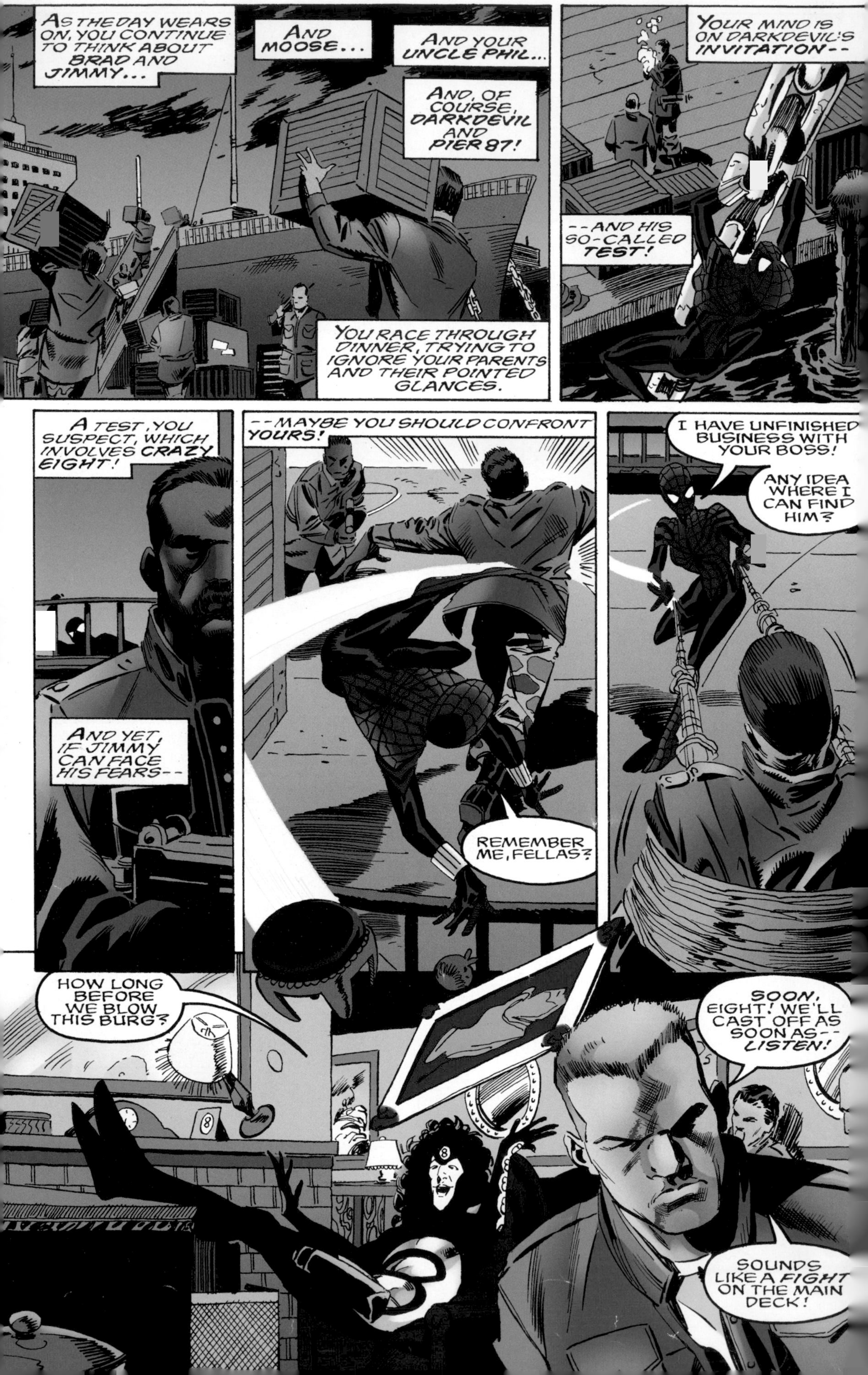
AS THE DAY WEARS ON, YOU CONTINUE TO THINK ABOUT BRAD AND JIMMY...
AND MOOSE...
AND YOUR UNCLE PHIL...
AND, OF COURSE, DARKDEVIL AND PIER 87!
YOU RACE THROUGH DINNER, TRYING TO IGNORE YOUR PARENTS AND THEIR POINTED GLANCES.
YOUR MIND IS ON DARKDEVIL'S INVITATION--
--AND HIS SO-CALLED TEST!
A TEST, YOU SUSPECT, WHICH INVOLVES CRAZY EIGHT!
AND YET, IF JIMMY CAN FACE HIS FEARS--
--MAYBE YOU SHOULD CONFRONT YOURS!
REMEMBER ME, FELLAS?
I HAVE UNFINISHED BUSINESS WITH YOUR BOSS!
ANY IDEA WHERE I CAN FIND HIM?
HOW LONG BEFORE WE BLOW THIS BURG?
SOON, EIGHT! WE'LL CAST OFF AS SOON AS--LISTEN!
SOUNDS LIKE A FIGHT ON THE MAIN DECK!

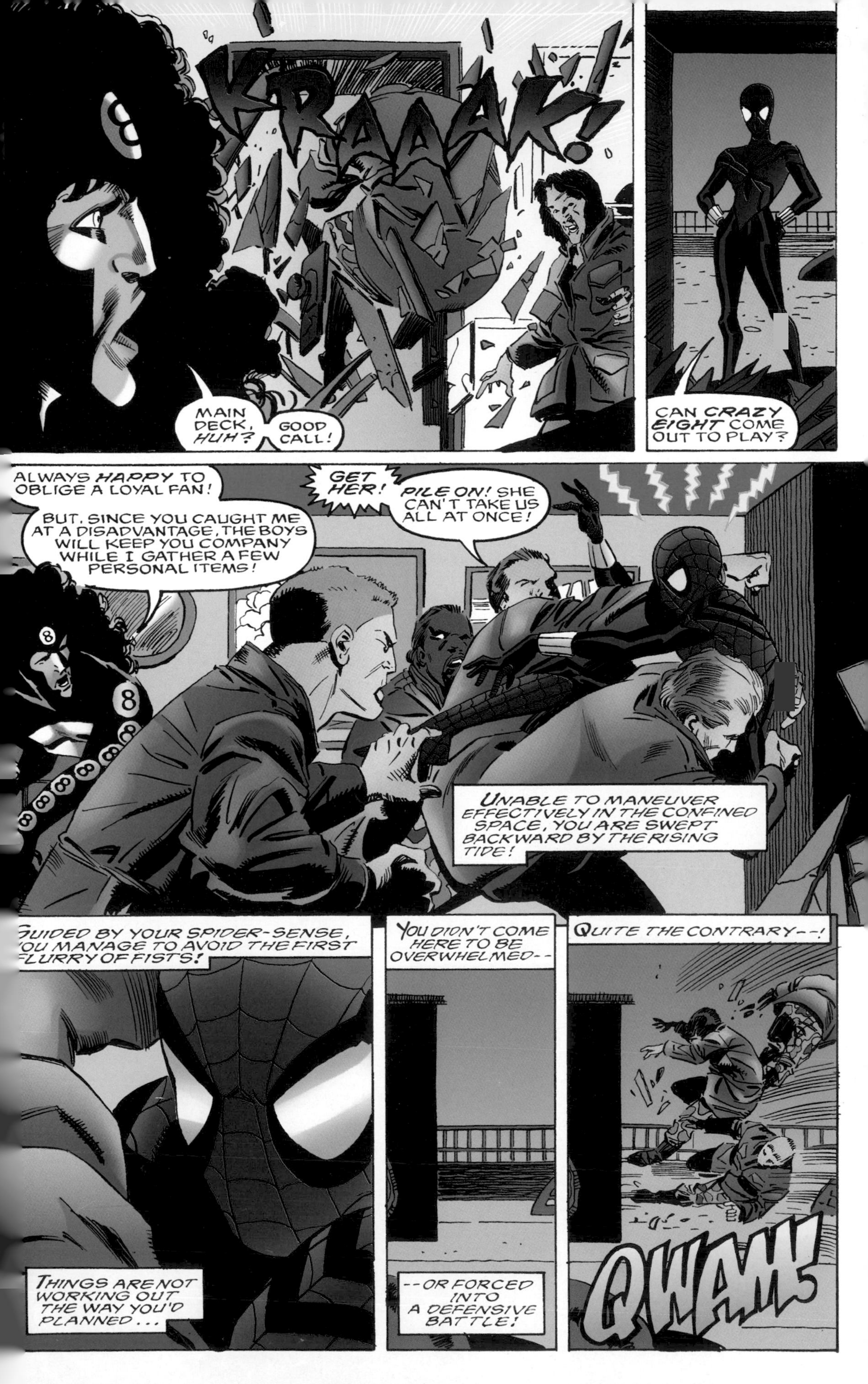
KRAAAK!
MAIN DECK, HUH?
GOOD CALL!
CAN CRAZY EIGHT COME OUT TO PLAY?
ALWAYS HAPPY TO OBLIGE A LOYAL FAN!
BUT, SINCE YOU CAUGHT ME AT A DISADVANTAGE, THE BOYS WILL KEEP YOU COMPANY WHILE I GATHER A FEW PERSONAL ITEMS!
GET HER!
PILE ON! SHE CAN'T TAKE US ALL AT ONCE!
UNABLE TO MANEUVER EFFECTIVELY IN THE CONFINED SPACE, YOU ARE SWEPT BACKWARD BY THE RISING TIDE!
GUIDED BY YOUR SPIDER-SENSE, YOU MANAGE TO AVOID THE FIRST FLURRY OF FISTS!
THINGS ARE NOT WORKING OUT THE WAY YOU'D PLANNED...
YOU DIDN'T COME HERE TO BE OVERWHELMED--
--OR FORCED INTO A DEFENSIVE BATTLE!
QUITE THE CONTRARY--!
QWAM!

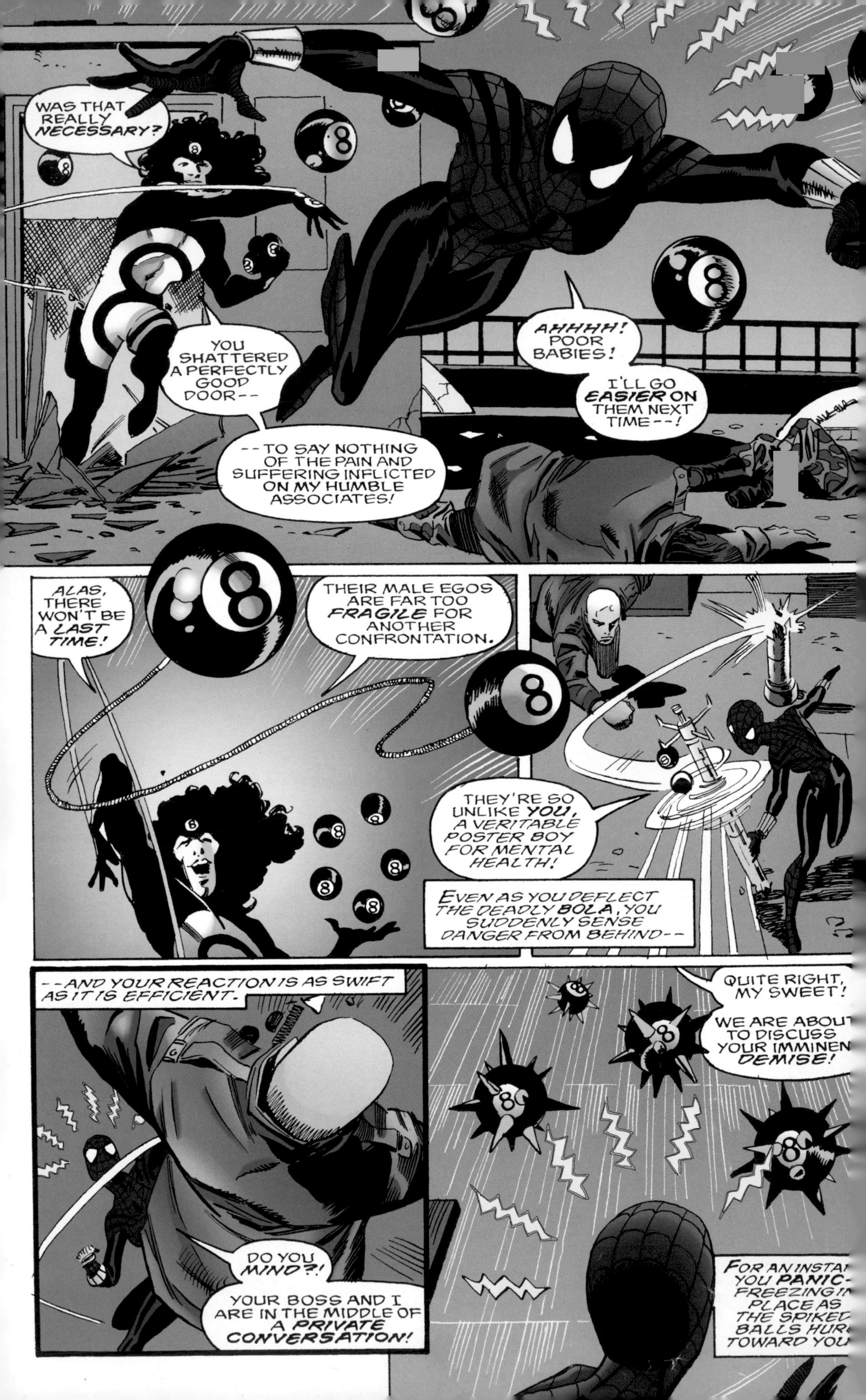

WAS THAT REALLY NECESSARY?
YOU SHATTERED A PERFECTLY GOOD DOOR--
--TO SAY NOTHING OF THE PAIN AND SUFFERING INFLICTED ON MY HUMBLE ASSOCIATES!
AHHHH! POOR BABIES!
I'LL GO EASIER ON THEM NEXT TIME--!
ALAS, THERE WON'T BE A LAST TIME!
THEIR MALE EGOS ARE FAR TOO FRAGILE FOR ANOTHER CONFRONTATION.
THEY'RE SO UNLIKE YOU, A VERITABLE POSTER BOY FOR MENTAL HEALTH!
EVEN AS YOU DEFLECT THE DEADLY BOLA, YOU SUDDENLY SENSE DANGER FROM BEHIND--
--AND YOUR REACTION IS AS SWIFT AS IT IS EFFICIENT.
DO YOU MIND?!
YOUR BOSS AND I ARE IN THE MIDDLE OF A PRIVATE CONVERSATION!
QUITE RIGHT, MY SWEET!
WE ARE ABOUT TO DISCUSS YOUR IMMINEN DEMISE!
FOR AN INSTA YOU PANIC- FREEZING IN PLACE AS THE SPIKED BALLS HUR TOWARD YOU

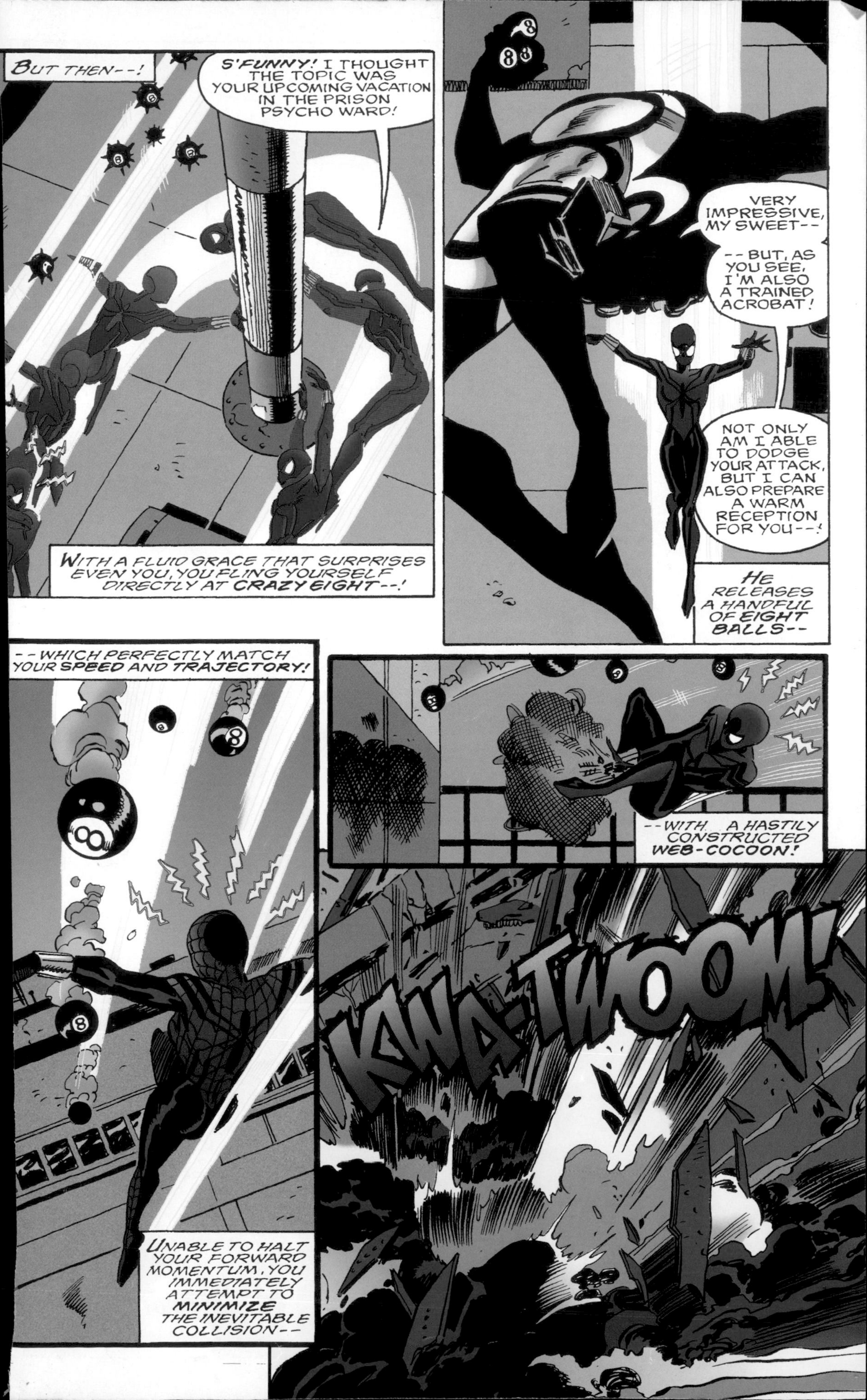
BUT THEN--!
S'FUNNY! I THOUGHT THE TOPIC WAS YOUR UPCOMING VACATION IN THE PRISON PSYCHO WARD!
WITH A FLUID GRACE THAT SURPRISES EVEN YOU, YOU FLING YOURSELF DIRECTLY AT CRAZY EIGHT--!
VERY IMPRESSIVE, MY SWEET--
--BUT, AS YOU SEE, I'M ALSO A TRAINED ACROBAT!
NOT ONLY AM I ABLE TO DODGE YOUR ATTACK, BUT I CAN ALSO PREPARE A WARM RECEPTION FOR YOU--!
HE RELEASES A HANDFUL OF EIGHT BALLS--
--WHICH PERFECTLY MATCH YOUR SPEED AND TRAJECTORY!
UNABLE TO HALT YOUR FORWARD MOMENTUM, YOU IMMEDIATELY ATTEMPT TO MINIMIZE THE INEVITABLE COLLISION--
--WITH A HASTILY CONSTRUCTED WEB-COCOON!
KWA-TWOOM!

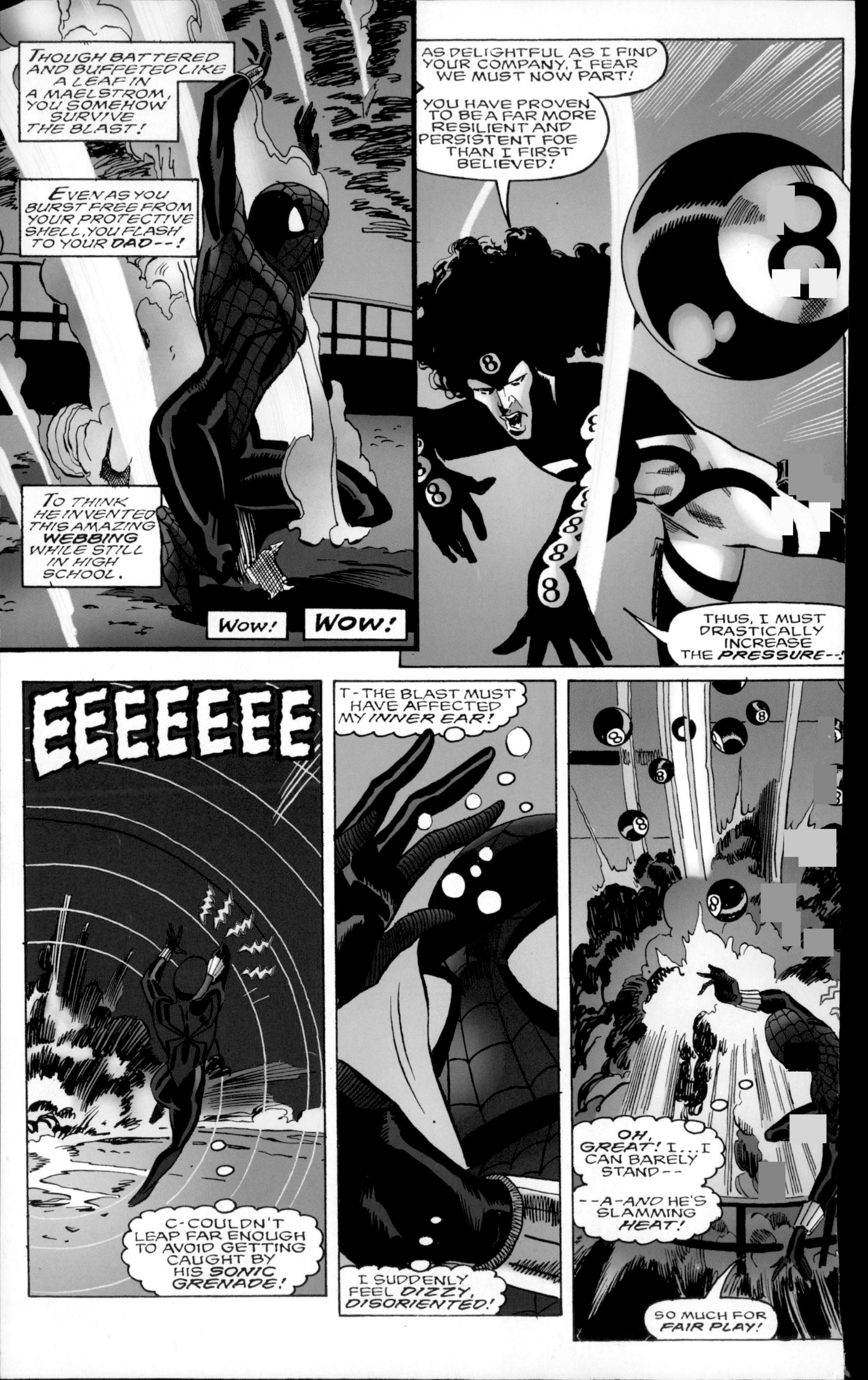
THOUGH BATTERED AND BUFFETED LIKE A LEAF IN A MAELSTROM, YOU SOMEHOW SURVIVE THE BLAST!
EVEN AS YOU BURST FREE FROM YOUR PROTECTIVE SHELL, YOU FLASH TO YOUR DAD--!
TO THINK HE INVENTED THIS AMAZING WEBBING WHILE STILL IN HIGH SCHOOL.
WOW!
WOW!
AS DELIGHTFUL AS I FIND YOUR COMPANY, I FEAR WE MUST NOW PART!
YOU HAVE PROVEN TO BE A FAR MORE RESILIENT AND PERSISTENT FOE THAN I FIRST BELIEVED!
THUS, I MUST DRASTICALLY INCREASE THE PRESSURE--!
EEEEEEE
C-COULDN'T LEAP FAR ENOUGH TO AVOID GETTING CAUGHT BY HIS SONIC GRENADE!
T-THE BLAST MUST HAVE AFFECTED MY INNER EAR!
I SUDDENLY FEEL DIZZY, DISORIENTED!
OH, GREAT! I...I CAN BARELY STAND--
--A-AND HE'S SLAMMING HEAT!
SO MUCH FOR FAIR PLAY!

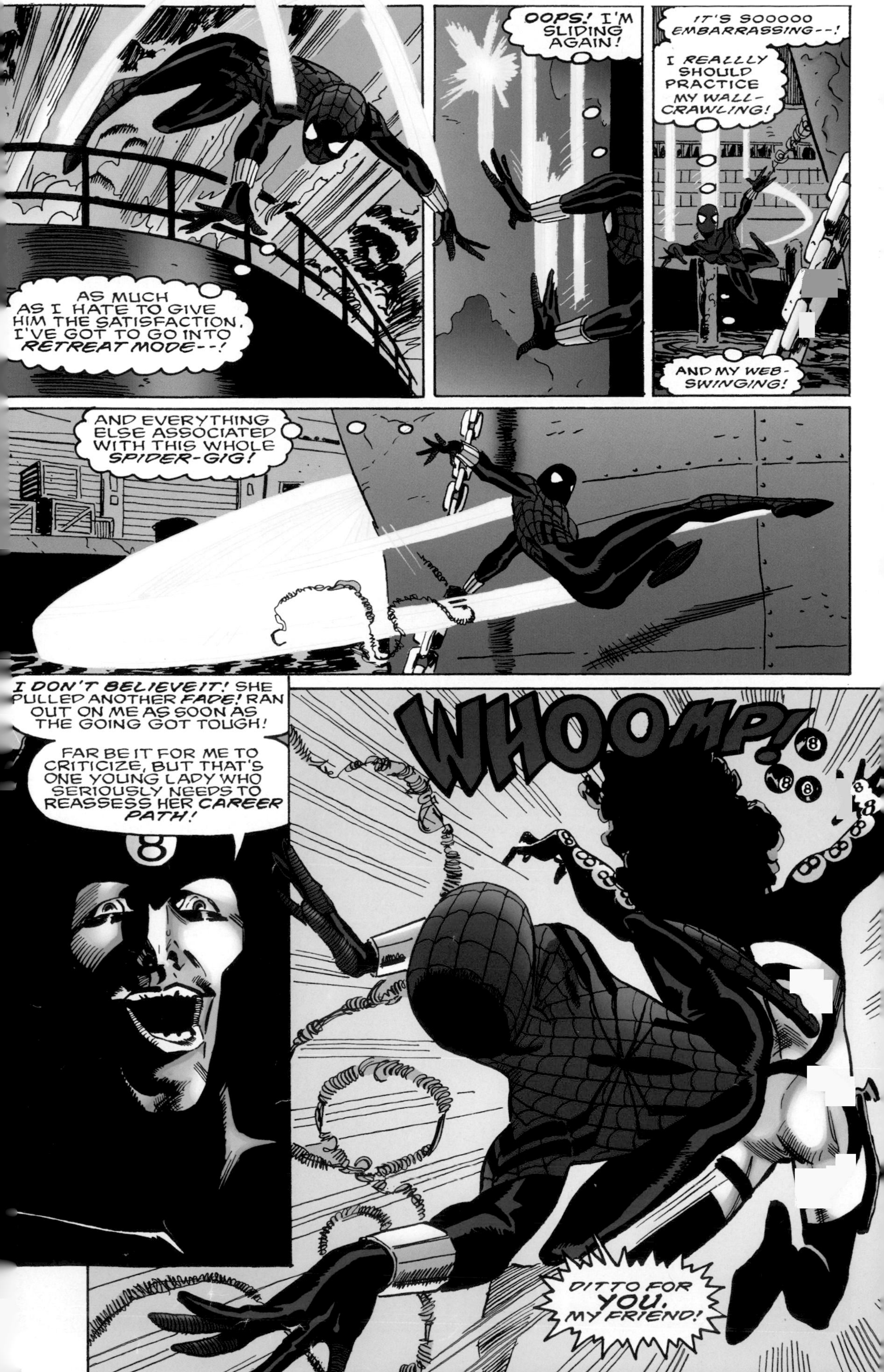
AS MUCH AS I HATE TO GIVE HIM THE SATISFACTION, I'VE GOT TO GO INTO RETREAT MODE--!
OOPS! I'M SLIDING AGAIN!
IT'S SOOOOOO EMBARRASSING--!
I REALLLY SHOULD PRACTICE MY WALL-CRAWLING!
AND MY WEB-SWINGING!
AND EVERYTHING ELSE ASSOCIATED WITH THIS WHOLE SPIDER-GIG!
I DON'T BELIEVE IT! SHE PULLED ANOTHER FADE! RAN OUT ON ME AS SOON AS THE GOING GOT TOUGH!
FAR BE IT FOR ME TO CRITICIZE, BUT THAT'S ONE YOUNG LADY WHO SERIOUSLY NEEDS TO REASSESS HER CAREER PATH!
WHOOMP!
DITTO FOR YOU, MY FRIEND!

A WIDE GRIN GLOWS BENEATH YOUR MASK AS YOU MENTALLY CHALK IN THE WIN!

CRAZY EIGHT UNDERESTIMATED YOU, NEVER SUSPECTING THAT YOU WERE CIRCLING BEHIND HIM!

ARROGANCE CERTAINLY HAS A NASTY HABIT OF LEADING TO DEFEAT!

YOU--!

I WAS WONDERING WHEN YOU'D SHOW!

FEELING PROUD OF YOURSELF, LITTLE GIRL?

ENJOY YOUR VICTORY... FOR WHATEVER IT'S WORTH!

WHAT'S YOUR DEAL, ANYWAY? WHY ARE YOU HASSLING ME?

I'M MERELY TRYING TO FORESTALL AN UNNECESSARY FUNERAL, KID!

YOU WERE EXCEPTIONALLY LUCKY TONIGHT!

BUT LUCK DOESN'T LAST!

NEITHER DO THOSE WHO PLAY AT BEING A HERO!

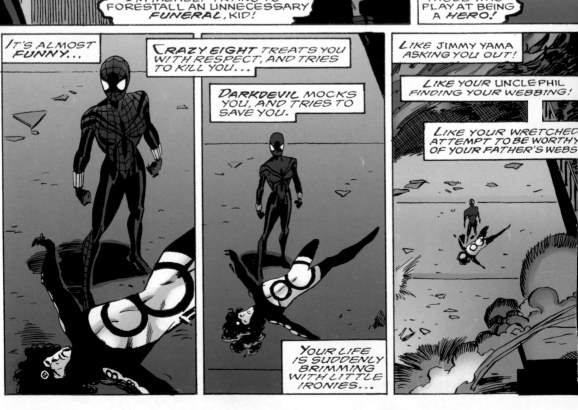

IT'S ALMOST FUNNY...

CRAZY EIGHT TREATS YOU WITH RESPECT, AND TRIES TO KILL YOU...

DARKDEVIL MOCKS YOU, AND TRIES TO SAVE YOU.

YOUR LIFE IS SUDDENLY BRIMMING WITH LITTLE IRONIES...

LIKE JIMMY YAMA ASKING YOU OUT!

LIKE YOUR UNCLE PHIL FINDING YOUR WEBBING!

LIKE YOUR WRETCHED ATTEMPT TO BE WORTHY OF YOUR FATHER'S WEBS!